W9-BEO-263

XINGU

XINGU

BY VIOLETTE AND JOHN VIERTEL

Pictures by *KARLA KUSKIN*

THE MACMILLAN COMPANY, New York

Library of Congress catalog card number: 59–5343

First Printing

The Macmillan Company, New York
Brett-Macmillan Ltd., Galt, Ontario

PRINTED IN THE UNITED STATES OF AMERICA

For Valérie

Long before the first men from Europe sailed to America, a little boy named Xingu lived in the valley of the Amazon in Brazil. The Amazon is one of the greatest rivers in the world and it runs from the high Andes Mountains across almost the whole South American continent to the Atlantic Ocean. It runs right along the equator, through an unending jungle forest.

Xingu was an Indian boy, for before the Europeans came, all the people of South America were Indians, and he lived with his parents in a hut in the jungle. His father Japura had made a clearing by burning down the great trees, and there Xingu's parents had built their hut, with slender tree trunks to hold up the roof, which slanted down almost to the ground, and thatched with palm leaves to keep out the water. For in the valley of the Amazon it rains almost every day. And just a little way from the clearing and the hut flowed the broad and muddy river.

In that strange and wonderful country, Xingu grew up under the care and love of his parents, and became a strong and cheerful boy. When he had learned to walk, his father took him to the bank of the great river, so that Xingu could watch him fish. Japura stood in his canoe, which he had made from a large tree trunk hollowed out, and held in his hand the trident, the three pointed spear, and watched for the fish beneath the surface. When he saw a nice large one, he would strike with the trident with lightning speed, and spear the fish in the water.

But when his father went hunting in the jungle, little Xingu had to stay with his mother at the hut. Xingu would watch his father take the strong curved bow, and rub fat on the string, and prepare the arrows, sharpening the points and binding the feathers onto the end of the shaft. Xingu would watch all this, and filled with curiosity, would ask his father to take him hunting too, but Japura would reply: "Not yet, little Xingu. When you grow older, you can come with me, but not now—Hunting is for men."

So Xingu had to stay behind with his mother, playing in the hut and in the small clearing. And as he grew older he also began to help his mother with her work—help her make the flour, called cassava, which was made from the manioc root, or to clean and dress the skins of the animals which Japura brought back from hunting, or to make a new hammock of netted palm fibres —for they slept in hammocks hung from the poles of their hut.

Xingu always played alone, for he had no brothers and sisters, and his parents lived by themselves in the jungle. There was a village of his father's tribe on down the river, but his father preferred to live out in the jungle, away from the others, for he said that in this way he found more game for his arrows, and more fish for his spear. Only rarely did he go to the village, which was half a day's journey away.

One day Japura took Xingu with him when he went to the village. They set out very early in the morning, going down the river in the dugout canoe. For the jungle was too thick, with vines and creepers growing between the tree trunks, to travel through it for any distance. So longer journeys were always made by water on the river.

Xingu sat in the bow of the canoe, watching the green

banks slip by, while his father sat back in the stern, paddling with smooth and powerful strokes. The water gurgled quietly along the sides of the canoe, and they went swiftly downstream. Xingu was very excited, and watched everything around him, so that he would be sure not to miss anything, for he had never been on such a great journey before.

Then, after they had been traveling for what seemed like a very long time, his father turned the canoe in toward the bank. They stepped ashore, and Japura pulled the canoe out of the water, and hid it in the undergrowth. The jungle seemed just as thick and impenetrable here as anywhere along the river, and Xingu wondered where the village might be. "The trail begins farther back," his father explained. "It is a secret trail, and only the members of our tribe know how to find it —that is so enemy tribes cannot come to our village."

They pushed on through the dense jungle till they came to a narrow twisting trail. They followed that a little while till it ended as suddenly as it had begun. Then they went through dense unbroken jungle again.

Finally they came to the clearing. It was much larger than the clearing in which Xingu's hut stood. In the middle was a great house of thatched palm leaves, as large as a circus tent, and very much the same shape. All the members of the tribe lived together in this house.

4

The men of the tribe greeted Japura, and took them into the great hut. Each family had its own place along the walls partitioned off by mats of palm leaves, and they had their hammocks and pots and other possessions and their own fire there. In the center of the hut was a large open space, which was used for ceremonies and tribal meetings and dancing.

While Japura went to the chief, to give him the game he had brought as a present, the children of the tribe gathered around Xingu. He had never thought that there were so many children in all the world. They stood around him in a circle, and stared at him. Xingu felt a little frightened with so many strange eyes on him. Finally a boy, who was a little older than the others, came up to him: "Who are you?" he asked.

"I am Xingu, the son of Japura," Xingu replied, trying to make his voice sound strong and firm, for he did not want them to know that he was frightened— "I live up the river with my father and my mother in the jungle—"

Finally one of the children said: "Come and play a game with us—" And another cried: "What game shall we play?" And a third boy said: "Let's play the hunting game." Then the first boy said: "Come, strange boy from the jungle, come and play the hunting game with us."

But Xingu looked down at the ground, very ashamed, and said: "I do not know how to play the hunting game—"

Then the others were very astonished, and cried: "You do not know the game, you do not know about hunting?"

And Xingu said, very softly: "No—"

Then the other children laughed at him and pointed at him, crying: "He does not know how to play, he does not know about hunting, isn't he a stupid boy!"

And still laughing, they ran off to play in the clearing, and left Xingu standing there alone. And he was very sad and ashamed, and stood very quietly in a corner of the great hut, looking out from time to time longingly at the children playing in the clearing, and waited till his father was ready to take him home.

On the way back Xingu sat very quietly in the canoe, till his father asked him what was wrong. Then Xingu told his father how the other children had laughed at him because he knew nothing of their games, and nothing about hunting— "But how can I know," he complained, "when I am always left behind with my mother? I am older now, almost eight years old, can't you take me with you now, father, so that I can learn about these things, please, father?"

But Japura, his father, said: "No, little Xingu, not

yet— You must not mind the others, my son, they are only silly children, and their games are not important. In a few years, you can come with me, and then I will teach you how to be a real hunter, and how to track through the forest, and how to shoot straight and true, and then all those who laughed at you will envy you, and will treat you with respect. But you will have to wait till it is time—and you have to learn to be patient. For that is the first thing a hunter must learn—how to wait and be patient."

That night Xingu could not sleep. The day had been too full of adventures and new things: the voyage down the river, the big hut of the tribe, and the meeting with the children, all that kept going around in Xingu's mind as he lay in his hammock in the dark hut. And again and again he would hear the jeering and the laughter of the other children, and see them standing in a circle around him, pointing their fingers at him.

And the next day Xingu was restless and bad tempered. And he was no help to his mother, though she had many things to do in the hut. He was always getting in her way, and asking her questions, till she finally became impatient with him—"Go and play," she told him, "go and play in the clearing."

But Xingu said: "How can I play, when I have no one to play with? All the children in the tribe have children to play with, but I have no one. How can I play —I do not even know the games."

Then his mother was sad and did not know what to reply. For it was true, they lived alone in the jungle, and they had not given him any little brothers and sisters to play with. He had been happy enough by himself, until he had gone to the village of the tribe. But now, because he had seen other children, he understood for the first time what being alone meant.

Finally his mother said quietly: "Go and watch the fish in the river, Xingu—"

And Xingu went down to the river, and sat down on the bank, and looked sadly into the water.

And though he tried during all the days after that, to be patient and to wait, like his father had told him— and kept saying to himself all the time: "I must learn to be patient if I want to be a great hunter—" Still he could no longer be happy playing by himself as he had been before.

Then one morning his father was again preparing to go out hunting. Taking his bow and his arrows, he said to Xingu: "Now you will be a good boy, and stay here and help your mother till I return in the evening."

And Xingu said: "Yes, father."

But when Japura left, Xingu looked after him, and watched him go toward the river. And when his mother turned to push the logs closer into the fire, Xingu ran quickly out of the hut, and ran after his father.

He could still see Japura ahead—his father was walking along the river bank, swinging along with great steady strides. And though Xingu tried to go fast too, he was getting out of breath, and could not keep up with his father. And he saw his father's figure getting smaller and smaller ahead.

Then suddenly Japura turned off to one side, and in an instant had disappeared into the forest. And when Xingu came to the place where his father had turned off, he could see nothing at all—only the tree trunks growing thicker and thicker together, and the strong creepers hanging like green ropes between them, and the dark green leaves of the undergrowth. He took a few steps in the direction he thought his father had taken, and suddenly the forest seemed to close in all around him, on every side were walls of thick vegetation, and the harsh cries of the birds, and the chattering of the monkeys, which had sounded so familiar and harmless at home in the clearing, was now coming from everywhere, and so near and so loud that it frightened him.

Xingu turned quickly, and he was very glad when he could still see the water shimmering through the trees, and he ran back to the river—

But then he stopped abruptly—for there, lying right

in his path, was a strange animal, an animal he had never seen before. And on the one side was the broad muddy river, and on the other the dense dark trees, and in front of him lay the strange animal, blocking his path back to the hut. Xingu looked to the right, and to the left, and did not know which way to go.

Then the animal looked up at him and said: "Don't be afraid—I am Liniani, the vicuña." And the animal spoke with such a gentle voice that Xingu was no longer afraid, and came nearer, looking at it full of wonder—

"But I have never seen anyone like you before!" Xingu said. "Where do you come from?"

Then Liniani the vicuña replied: "My family and all the other vicuñas live high up in the mountains, where the fierce winds blow and the snow lies on the ground all year. But I was always cold up there, my fur was just not as thick as that of my parents and my brothers and sisters and all the other vicuñas. At first they laughed at me when I said I was cold, and told me that no vicuña had ever been cold up in the mountains, even when there was snow and ice everywhere. But then they saw that, truly, my fur was not growing as thick and proper as it should, and my parents became more and more worried about me—for I shivered and cried all the time. Finally they said to me: 'You must go down from the cold mountains, my child, and live in the valleys below, in the hot pampas, and the steaming forest by the great river, and there you will no longer be cold.' So early one morning I left them, to journey down, far down into the low country. And my parents and all my brothers stood on the top of the mountain and waved good-bye to me, and shouted: 'Good luck!' And so I came down to live in the warm forest by the river."

Meanwhile the sun had climbed high in the sky. And Xingu heard, far in the distance, his mother's voice calling. She was calling for him anxiously, she was worried because she could not find him anywhere near the hut.

Then Xingu said to the vicuña: "O, I must go quickly, for it is lunchtime, and my mother, whose voice you hear, is calling me. She seems to be worried, for she cannot find me, and I must hurry home quickly."

Then the vicuña said: "Jump on my back, Xingu, and hold onto my neck, and you will be home in no time at all."

Xingu climbed on the vicuña's back, and held on tightly, as he had been told, and they went swiftly as the wind, till they came to where the high grass ended, at the edge of the clearing. There the vicuña stopped and said, turning his head to Xingu: "I do not want to go further than the high grass, because I do not want them to see me—" and he knelt so Xingu could get off.

"But shall I meet you again?" Xingu asked the vicuña anxiously.

"Yes," Liniani replied, "I will meet you here tomorrow morning, and then we will go into the jungle together."

Then Xingu was so happy that he was singing and dancing all the way back to the hut.

His mother asked him where he had been, for he had been gone since early morning. But Xingu thought it better to say nothing of his secret adventure, and of his new friend, so he only said: "O, down by the river, watching the fish."

All afternoon he helped his mother so well and cheerfully, as he had never done before, because he was so happy, and looking forward to the next morning with such expectancy. She was making cassava from manioc roots.

Now manioc is the main food of the Indians of the Amazon. But it has a poison in it, and they must prepare it very carefully in order to draw all the poison out. Xingu's mother had first soaked the roots for a long time, and some of the poison was drawn out by that. Then she grated it on a grater made of a wooden board set with the sharp spines of the palms. For the Indians had no metal and very few stones, so they had to make their tools and utensils out of palms and trees, and the bones of animals and their teeth, and also the sharp teeth of the piranha fish.

She had grated all the roots now, and then Xingu helped her pack the pulp into a long tube, made of palm leaves woven together. This tube was made in such a way, that if you pulled on the ends it would get narrower, and squeeze the grated roots packed inside it tightly. Xingu's mother hung one end of the tube to the roof pole of the hut, and put a strong stick through the loop at the other end. Then she and Xingu sat on the stick, and their weight pulled the tube until it squeezed the manioc roots very tight and all the juice was squeezed out. Then they took the pulp out and laid it in the sun to dry. Then it would have to be heated and stirred in a pot, till all the rest of the poison was cooked out of it. Finally it was dried again, till it became a flour that could be baked into a hard dry bread. The flour was called cassava.

This was very hard work, as can easily be imagined, and Xingu's mother was happy that he helped her so well.

And in the evening, after his father had come home, and after Xingu had gone to sleep in his hammock, his mother said to his father Japura: "He was a very good boy today, he helped me all afternoon with my work, and he seemed much more cheerful and happy than he has been since the day he went to the village."

Japura was glad to hear that, and said: "Yes, he is growing up, he is growing up quickly now, soon I shall have to start to teach him the things that a man must know."

The next morning Xingu woke up very early, and as soon as he opened his eyes he was filled with an eager happiness—for this morning he was going to meet his new friend. He could hardly wait till they had drunk the hot drink made of herbs, which was their usual breakfast, and till his father had gone off to hunt. Then he called to his mother: "I am going to play by the river." And he ran off as quickly as he could.

Liniani the vicuña was already waiting for him at the clearing's edge—

"Where shall we go, Xingu?" asked the vicuña.

"Why I do not know," said Xingu. "You see, I have never really been anywhere. Once my father took me to the village down the river, but that is the only place I have ever been."

"Would you like to go into the forest?" asked the vicuña.

"O yes," said Xingu eagerly, "I should like that very much."

"Get onto my back then," said the vicuña, "and let us be off."

Xingu jumped on the vicuña's back, and they went off, as fast as the egret flies—and he clung tightly onto Liniani's neck, so that he should not fall off, for they were going so fast.

They went for a while through the jungle, and then they came to the edge of the forest, where the plains, the pampas, begin. There were low rolling hills there, and they came to one hill a little higher than all the others, and there they stopped for a moment at its summit. Sitting high on the vicuña's back, Xingu could see everything for miles around, as he had never seen it before:

the jungle forest stretching out to the one side, and the great river winding through the trees, shining silvery grey in the dark green foliage, and on the other side, the rolling plains stretched out, all yellow, for the hot sun had burned the grass dry till it was a golden color. And beyond that, rising high to the sky, was a huge jagged wall, purple and blue in the distance. It stretched all the way across the horizon, and did not seem to have any end. And on the highest points there was gleaming white—

"What is that?" asked Xingu.

"Those are the mountains, the Andes," replied the vicuña— "Up there was my home."

"And what is that white gleaming at the top?" asked Xingu.

"That is the snow," said Liniani, and shivered a little, just at the memory.

"Snow—" said Xingu. "What is snow like?" For he had never in his life seen snow, living in the jungle of the Amazon, where it never snows at all—

"It is very white, as you see, and wet, when you touch it, and it can be soft as feathers, or hard as stone when it is packed, and cold—you cannot imagine how cold!"

Xingu looked at the high mountains and the snow a little while longer, full of amazement, and then they went on.

Now they entered the jungle forest, the great tree trunks rising around them, their branches arching above, and the leaves shutting out the sky—

"You must be tired, carrying me all this way," said Xingu, for they had traveled a great distance.

"I am, a little," the vicuña admitted.

"Then I will get off and we will walk together," said Xingu, and scrambled off the animal's back.

They advanced slowly into the darkness of the jungle. At first Xingu was frightened and walked very close beside his friend. But gradually he became more accustomed to the strangeness of it, to the damp smells, to the sudden chattering of the monkeys, and the shrill cries of the birds directly over their heads, and the tangles of thick creepers and undergrowth that grew everywhere. And it was not nearly so frightening when you were with a friend who knew the way.

And Xingu began to scramble eagerly over the great gnarled roots of the trees that crossed the forest path, and ducking under low branches and creepers, he would run ahead and then wait for the vicuña to catch up with him. He was running ahead towards an especially thick tangle of vines, when suddenly he heard his friend calling him —and Liniani's voice was sharp and sounded very frightened: "Look out, look out, Xingu!"

Xingu turned and saw the vicuña standing quite still,

frozen in its tracks, staring at the thick tangle of jungle
growth ahead— "Don't go further, Xingu!"

Then Xingu looked where the vicuña had his eyes
fixed—and saw a thick, long, winding branch among
the creepers. And then he saw that it was strangely
smooth and spotted, and though it was quite still, it
didn't really look like a branch at all. Then suddenly
Xingu was very frightened. Slowly, softly, he backed
away, till he was beside his friend again—"What is it,
what is it, Liniani—" he whispered.

"Anaconda, the big snake—" the vicuña whispered back. "It lies quite still like that, so that one thinks it is just a big branch—and then when you get too close, suddenly it coils itself around you, quick as lightning, and then —Let us get away from here quickly."

So they turned, and at first went softly and quietly, glancing back over their shoulders, but when they were a little further away, ran as fast as they could—

After they had run a long ways Liniani stopped. "It is all right now, it will not chase us, it will just lie there and wait for something else to come along. You see, Xingu, that is one thing you must learn in the jungle, you must always keep your eyes open and look very closely at everything around you—and never dash off like you did, without first looking to see what is in front and above and on every side of you."

"Yes," said Xingu, "I shall certainly remember that, for I shall never forget the way that thing that was not a branch looked!"

"And what do we do now?" Xingu asked the vicuña.

"Let us go and meet one of my friends—it is just about his lunchtime, and I am quite sure I know where we shall find him."

The vicuña led the way through the forest, and Xingu remained close by his side now, and looked very carefully about him at every step. They came to a small open space between the trees—it was covered by many high cone shaped mounds, so that it looked like a group of miniature volcanoes all crowded together— "What is that?" asked Xingu.

"Those are the hills of the great ants. But let us wait here, hidden behind these trees, and soon my friend will come, and we can watch him get his lunch, for it is an interesting and amusing thing to see."

So they hid themselves behind the trees where the branches grew densely together, so that they could not be seen but could look out through the thick leaves. "Now we must wait quietly," whispered the vicuña, and so they crouched there, and Xingu hardly dared draw his breath, for he was trying to be as quiet as possible.

And after a little while they saw the leaves of the branches over the path move, and then the strangest looking animal came shuffling through the jungle. He had a very long thin head, with a nose that looked like a long tube, and his body was covered by thick bushy black hair tipped white at the end, and he was very large and had a tremendously long bushy tail. And he came shuffling along, walking on the sides of his fore feet, because these had such long sharp claws that he could not step down on them. And his long nose was snuffing the ground all the way as he came.

Xingu was somewhat frightened, so strange and gro-

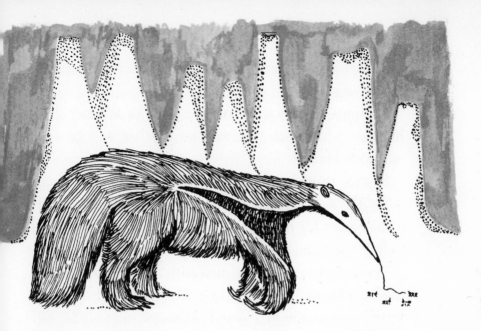

tesque did this large animal look, and he moved closer to the vicuña and looked at him questioningly. And Liniani said, to calm him: "Don't be afraid, Xingu, it is my friend. I admit that he looks somewhat strange and formidable, but he will not hurt us, and he is really a very nice fellow. But before we say hello to him, let us watch him a little—"

The strange beast now came to the ant hills. He stopped and sniffed them all over, very carefully, and then began to dig at them with his great sharp claws, burrowing very fast and throwing the earth behind him, till he was satisfied that he had dug deep enough into the heart of the ant hill—then he thrust his long snout into the ant hill.

23

"What is he doing?" Xingu asked, wondering at this strange sight—

"Eating—he eats ants. You see, he is an anteater. Let him finish his lunch in peace and then we will go and talk with him."

So they waited, and Xingu watched with fascination, while the anteater dug into several more ant hills—till he had eaten his fill. Then they stepped forth from their hiding place and greeted him—

"How do you do," the vicuña said, "I want you to meet a friend of mine: —this is Xingu who lives in a hut down by the river. —Xingu, I would like you to meet my friend the anteater—"

"How do you do," the anteater said to Xingu.

"Very well, thank you," Xingu replied, "and how are you, sir?"

"O I can't complain," the anteater said.

"I hope you had a good lunch," the vicuña said.

"Not bad, not bad at all," the anteater replied, with the visible satisfaction of one who has just had a good meal—and then added with gracious courtesy: "If you would care for some? They are really very tasty ants, and I should be happy to dig some up for you."

"It is very kind of you," the vicuña said, "but I'm afraid that my friend and I do not have such a refined palate, we have not developed a taste for ants."

24

"You should try them—perhaps you will not like them so well the first time, but after the second or the third, they grow on you, and you will agree with me that they are quite a delicacy. And these—" he said, pointing to the ant hills, "are really quite choice."

The vicuña looked at Xingu questioningly, and seeing the rather troubled look on his face, said quickly: "It is really very kind of you—another time perhaps. But as we speak of lunch," Liniani went on, turning to Xingu, "isn't it near your lunchtime too, Xingu? We had better hurry home now, for if your mother misses you and grows worried, then the next time it might be more difficult for you to come out with me. It is always best, I think, to be home in time for lunch."

Xingu agreed that his friend was right, though he was very reluctant to leave, having just met such an interesting new acquaintance as the anteater. So sadly he said good-bye to him, and that he hoped he might meet him again soon, to which the anteater replied that he hoped so too.

On the way home Xingu said to Liniani: "You are quite right about your friend—he is really nice, after one grows used to his frightening appearance."

"Yes," said the vicuña, "that is the way it is with many people one meets. And, of course, to him we probably look just as strange as he does to us."

Xingu arrived home just as his mother was finishing preparing the lunch. He ate with great appetite, for he was very hungry from his long journey. And he was so happy because he had a friend now, and such exciting adventures, that he felt full of strength and life and joy, and he just had to do something. So, after lunch, when his mother brought out the wooden bowl, to pound some more cassava meal, he told her that he would do that today. So he pounded the meal, and worked hard all afternoon, and when he had finished that, he went to fetch a log of wood for the fire.

The Indians make fire by turning a thin reed against a piece of wood with a small hollow in it. But it is so damp in the jungle, that it is very difficult to start a fire that way, and therefore they try to keep the fire burning all the time. They lay down three logs with the burning ends pointing into the center of the fire, and push them in closer as they burn. And when one of the logs is burned very short, they fetch another to put in its place. Thus Xingu did the work in the hut that afternoon. And his mother could sit quietly and finish the new hammock she was weaving of tucum palm leaves, which she had been working on for a long time. And while she was weaving, the mother looked at her son, working so full of energy and happiness, and so she was happy too, thinking what a fine boy her son was growing up to be.

And every day Liniani the vicuña would be waiting
for his friend Xingu in the morning, in the high grass at
the clearing's edge, and they would go off together to
play in the jungle. And the vicuña introduced Xingu to
many of the animals that roamed wild there, and taught
him all the secrets of the forest: how to distinguish the
faintest sound and tell what had made it and why; how
to read the tracks on the ground and tell from them
who had been there and when and what they had done.
And he showed him the favorite feeding places of the
various animals, and which berries were sweet and good

27

to eat, and warned him of those which would make him ill, and showed him the watering places, where the water was pure and good to drink. Soon little Xingu knew more of the secret lore of the jungle than even his father, who was a great hunter, did.

Then one day Liniani said to Xingu: "We shall visit two of my friends, for there has been a great event: they have just had seven little children, so all of us are going there this morning to congratulate them, and to bring them gifts."

And Xingu said: "Yes, you told me yesterday that we would, and I have remembered, I have brought a basket of cassava meal for them."

So they set out. And on their way through the forest they met the armadillo, which is a most curious animal all covered with plates of armor. Liniani told the armadillo that they were on their way to visit friends who had just had seven little ones. And the armadillo said he would come with them too— "But what sort of a gift can I bring them, I have nothing, and I really should bring a gift."

"They will be very happy to see you, even if you don't bring anything," said Xingu.

"But it would not be the polite thing to do," the armadillo objected.

But now they stopped, for they had come to the place

where the vicuña had hidden his present, which he fetched now. It was a large branch with bunches of sweet berries on it. "Let us divide these berries, there are plenty," Liniani said to the armadillo. "And half will be my present, and the other half yours." The armadillo was happy with that arrangement and thanked the vicuña.

"Put the berries in my basket," Xingu said. "They will be easier to carry through the jungle that way."

So they put the berries in Xingu's basket, and continued on their way. And as they went farther, Xingu saw another friend of theirs. Now this friend was an animal called the sloth, because he is such a lazy animal. He has four hands which are no good at all for walking on the ground, but very good for grasping, and therefore also good for climbing. And he is an arboreal animal, that is, an animal which lives in the trees, like the monkeys do. The sloth spends most of his time hanging upside down from the branches by his four hands, and he is grey and has long hair, so that he looks just like one of the many bunches of spanish moss that hang from the trees in the jungle, making them look as if they had beards. And therefore it is very difficult to distinguish the sloth hanging in the branches, but Xingu's eyes had become very sharp by now, and so he recognized him and called up to him: "O sleepy friend, wake up! We are going to visit our friends who have just had seven little ones, to congratulate them and bring them gifts. Come with us!"

But the sloth said, yawning very widely: "I've only been sleeping since yesterday afternoon, I've just barely shut my eyes— You go along, and I'll come and join you after a little while, after I've had a bit more rest, for I am very tired."

But Xingu knew that if the sloth did not come with them right now, he would sleep on for another week. "No, no, you must come with us. And I'll tell you what, there are some very fine looking nuts in that tree right next to you, why don't you pick those and bring them along as a gift?"

But the sloth said: "They are very high in the tree."

Then the armadillo called up to him: That should be no trouble for one who climbs as well as you do!"

Then the sloth said: "Well, even if I pick them, how will I carry them?"

And Xingu said: "I will carry them for you."

And the sloth still did not move, but said: "They live such a long way off, it is really too far to go, climbing all the way through the trees, as I must—"

Then the vicuña said: "Very well, come down and get on my back and I will carry you too, but fetch down the nuts first."

So the sloth, after a great deal of yawning and rubbing his eyes, slowly climbed up, and he began to pluck the nuts, which he dropped down, one by one. Xingu caught them and put them in his basket.

"That is really a very practical invention, such a basket," said the armadillo admiringly.

When the sloth had thrown them a sufficient quantity of nuts, he slowly climbed down, and let himself drop from the lowest branch onto the vicuña's back. And so they went on, the four friends: the vicuña, the sloth, the armadillo and Xingu, through the forest.

They went deeper and deeper into the jungle, until they met the proud father, who was standing on the path, waiting for them. He was a peccary, which is a sort of wild pig that lives in the jungle, but being wild, he is slender, and not nearly so fat as a tame pig. "It is very nice of you to come," he said, as he greeted them. "I thought I would wait here and show you the way."

And with that he led them off the path into the dense jungle growth at one side. It was well that he had come to guide them, for the peccaries' lair was well hidden indeed, behind a thick screen of jungle vines, in a hollow under the trunk of a huge tree. There the mother peccary lay, looking down proudly and fondly at her newborn children: all seven of the little ones, lying in a row, nuzzling at their mother's side.

Several other friends were already there—the anteater, and the tapir, who is a distant relative of the elephant, but not nearly so large, and the brilliantly colored toucan bird, with his huge beak, was sitting on a branch above.

Xingu proudly brought out his basket with the presents and put it on the ground in front of the mother, and emptying it, said: "These berries are from Liniani, and the other half of them is from the armadillo—and these nuts my friend the sloth picked himself from the highest trees with a great deal of effort and trouble. And this cassava meal is from me."

Both the mother and the father peccary thanked them profusely, and said that these were very wonderful presents indeed. Then the guests admired the newborn children, and said how beautiful and strong and intelligent they looked, which made the mother and the father very proud and happy.

Then suddenly they noticed that an awful stillness had fallen over all the jungle—and it was broken only by the sudden high frightened chattering of some monkeys a little way off—and the scream of a trumpet bird, far away. Then utter stillness again. And without quite knowing why, they were all suddenly oppressed by a feeling of great fear.

"Something is happening," said the mother peccary in a frightened voice. "I can feel it, something very bad is coming!"

33

"Yes," said the tapir, lifting his short trunk into the air. "Yes, I can smell it, I can smell the big fear spreading through the jungle—"

And the vicuña pricked up his long slender ears and said: "Yes, I can hear it, I can hear the awful stillness coming closer—"

And the toucan bird said: "I shall go and scout out what it is." And he flew away, high above the trees and out of their sight, and they waited in silence for his return. And the little animals, the mother peccary and the vicuña were beginning to tremble in every limb—

Then the toucan bird came swiftly flying back, and had barely perched on the limb above them, when he cried out: "Jaguar! The jaguar is out hunting! The trumpet bird told me, and then I saw him myself, coming slinking down the trail—"

Then the animals were more frightened than ever, and the mother peccary whispered: "O what shall we do, what shall we do—"

And the father said: "We must take the little ones and fly quickly—"

But the mother said: "No, we could never run away quickly enough with my seven little children who cannot walk yet—"

Then the anteater, looking very wise down his long nose, said: "We must keep him away from your hiding place—we must lead him away from here. One of us must show himself and lure him away in another direction."

"But who can do that, who can expose himself to such danger?" asked the mother. "For if the jaguar sees you he will catch you surely!"

"I will," said the father peccary. "I am the father and I can run quickly, perhaps he shall not catch me."

"And I will help you," said the vicuña. "I can run even more quickly than you, and I will run across your trail, and confuse him, if he gets too close to you."

"And I will throw big nuts at him, and annoy him," said the sloth. "He is big and heavy and can never climb up into the highest branches like I can."

"And I will dig a deep hole by the path," said the armadillo, "and jump out when he is coming along, and if he tries to chase me, duck back into the hole."

"And I shall fly across his nose, and confuse him even more," said the toucan bird.

"But what can I do?" asked Xingu. "I cannot run so fast, or dig such a deep hole, and I cannot fly—"

All the animals had turned to look at him— "Yes, what can we do about Xingu?" asked the vicuña.

Then the sloth yawned, for all this was going to require a great deal of energy, and he felt tired just from thinking about it—and he said: "Why the boy must come up into the trees with me."

"But I do not know whether I can climb so high," said Xingu worried.

"O I will show you," the sloth reassured him.

"We had better start now," said the vicuña, "for he will soon be near."

"Well, let us find a good high tree," said the sloth and yawned again.

"But far from here!" said the father peccary. "No one must be near this place."

"O all right," said the sloth, and then to Xingu, "let us look for a tree farther away then. But you will carry me, boy?"

"Yes, I'll carry you," Xingu assured him.

So the sloth climbed on Xingu's back, and they started off, while the others quickly pulled the vines together in front of the peccaries' lair, so that it was completely hidden from view. Then they dispersed, all going in different directions.

Xingu and the sloth went quickly through the forest, and when they had gone quite a way, the sloth said: "I think this will be far enough, and that looks like a fine tree there—"

And indeed, before them stood one of the highest trees in all the forest. When they had come up beside it, the sloth sitting up on Xingu's neck, reached out with his long arm, and took hold of one of the thick creepers that wound around the great tree. He pulled himself up by it, and then climbing hand over hand, reached the lowest branch, which was already very high off the ground.

"See how it is done?" he called down to Xingu.

And Xingu said, "Yes," trying not to let his voice show how frightened he was. And he took hold of the creeper too, and began to pull himself up by his hands, winding his legs around it.

"Come on up, you're doing fine," the sloth called to him encouragingly— And then, much to his surprise, Xingu found himself sitting on the thick branch beside his friend.

"You see, it not difficult at all," said the sloth.

"No, not at all," said Xingu quite happily and looked down at the ground below. He had been looking up at the sloth all the time while he was climbing, and had not looked down before. But now when he saw the ground so far down below, his stomach suddenly felt hollow, and his head began to spin, and his knees to tremble.

"Perhaps it is better not to look down," said the sloth when he saw Xingu's face turning quite green.

"Yes, perhaps it is better," said Xingu.

The sloth gave him a moment to recover, and then said: "Now come on, up we go!"

"Up?" Xingu exclaimed— "Must we climb still higher?"

"O much higher," said the sloth— "We are only on the lowest branch, and the jaguar is a very good climber, he will leap up here without any trouble at all."

The thought of the jaguar renewed Xingu's strength, and so they started climbing again. The sloth moved slowly and deliberately, but each movement brought him onto a higher branch, and then he would stop till Xingu had followed him, climbing up along the path which the sloth showed him. They went up and up till it seemed that they would climb right up to the sky.

"Isn't this high enough?" Xingu asked anxiously after they had climbed a while.

"No," said the sloth, "the jaguar still could follow us up here. But he is very big and heavy, you see, many times as heavy as you or I, so we must climb up to where the branches will just barely carry us, and therefore will no longer be strong enough to support his great weight."

So they kept on climbing up through the branches of the great tree, which rose much higher than those around it. And when Xingu looked around he could look out over the tree tops of all the forest on every side. Then the sloth finally halted. "This will do," he said— "That really was a climb."

"It certainly was!" said Xingu, sitting on one slender branch, and holding very tightly onto another—the branches swayed under his weight, which at first gave him a rather sickening feeling, but they held him. The sloth was already hanging comfortably from the next branch by his four hands— "I do not care for this much exercise in a month, let alone all in one day," he said, "I really feel worn out, and I think I'll get a little sleep. Wake me when the jaguar comes." And with that the sloth shut his eyes and was fast asleep in a minute.

Xingu had not dared to look at the ground since they started climbing up from the lowest branch. Now he glanced down for just an instant—and his stomach rose and turned over inside him, so that he almost fell off his perch. The ground seemed so terribly far away, that everything down there, the creepers, the leaves of the undergrowth and the large tropical flowers looked so tiny— and the path on which they had come was a thin ribbon.

Then suddenly the toucan bird flew up, and sat down on the branch in front of him— "He is coming," the toucan bird whispered excitedly— "the jaguar is coming now!"

And he flew off again.

Xingu shook the sloth gently by the shoulder. "He is coming," he whispered, when the sloth finally opened his eyes. The sloth yawned and sleepily rubbed his face, and then they both peered down the jungle path along which the jaguar would approach. They sat quite still now, not daring to move, and the feeling of danger that was spreading through the forest seized hold of them.

Then Xingu suddenly heard a shrill, high chattering, right behind his neck, and he turned in fright, so quickly that he almost fell off his branch—but it was only a marmoset, sitting on the branch above the back of his head, chattering so excitedly that his white ears were wiggling — "There he is, there he is!" shrilled the marmoset.

Xingu looked down again—and at the far end of the path he saw the great spotted cat come slinking. His long arched tail was whipping nervously back and forth behind him, and the great muscles rippled at the shoulders under the smooth mottled fur, and his lips were drawn

back, showing the great gleaming fangs, and his yellow eyes were burning with a somber light. Closer and closer the jaguar came, to the place where, just off the path, the jungle growth screened the peccaries' lair—

Then suddenly the father peccary came leaping out right in front of the jaguar, running, running as fast as he could away from the lair— The jaguar tensed, just for an instant, and then, bounding swiftly with great long leaps, he was after him. The father peccary ran as fast as he could, he was running for his life—but not fast enough, for the jaguar was drawing closer to him with each leap. Now he was almost on top of him—

And then suddenly the vicuña broke out of the under-brush and leaped across the trail, right in front of the jaguar's nose. And the vicuña ran quickly to the right, and the father peccary ran quickly to the left— And the jaguar stopped quite still for a moment, not knowing which of them he should pursue.

And the father peccary kept running, dodging back and forth between the trees, while the vicuña stopped and looked back at the jaguar, to make sure that the jaguar would chase him, for he knew that the father peccary was tiring and could not run much farther. It was a tre-mendously brave thing to do, to stand still like that and look the dreadful jaguar straight in the face, when every-thing inside Liniani was shouting: "Run, run, Liniani, run faster than you have ever run in your life!" But the vicuña stood quite still, till he saw the jaguar crouch, gathering his muscles together, so that they were like tightly wound steel springs—and then suddenly he came pouncing after him.

Watching from his high perch in the tree, from which he could see everything, Xingu was filled with admiration for the courage of his friend—but also his heart was at the top of his throat with fear for his sake.

Now the vicuña had started to run, his slender form leaping gracefully over the roots of the jungle trees, nimble and swift as the wind—while the jaguar, with tremendous powerful leaps came bounding after him, his great shoulders and haunches catapulting him forward, his great jaws wide open as though to devour the distance itself. And no matter how swiftly the little vicuña ran, the jaguar raced just as fast, and then slowly he began drawing closer and closer—

And Xingu, watching from his high tree grew more and more frightened for his friend. They were running towards the tree now, the jaguar still drawing closer and closer to Liniani. At this point the sloth began to throw the nuts he picked off the branches around him. And Xingu, who had been hanging onto his perch with both hands for dear life, forgot his own fear of falling off, when he saw his friend Liniani in such great danger, and he began to pluck nuts too, and to throw them with all his might, no matter how perilously the branch on which he was sitting began to sway from his violent movements.

So a rain of nuts as hard as stones began to pelt the jaguar on face and chest. But he was very hungry, and with the vicuña so near, he would let nothing stop him. And no matter how much the nuts stung him, he just shook his head angrily, and kept on racing after the little animal, and hardly slowed down at all—

And Xingu grew still more frightened, for now it looked as though the jaguar would pounce right on poor Liniani's back with his very next leap—

Then suddenly a flash of bright colored feathers flashed through the air above the great cat— It was the toucan bird, and he streaked right across the jaguar's nose till it looked as though he were flying right into the gaping jaws with their long white fangs. And he flapped his wings in the jaguar's eyes, and then rose up into the air and was away again, before the jaguar had even fully realized what had happened—

High in the air the bright colored bird banked and turned, and then came diving back again. This time, as he shot past, he chopped at the jaguar's back with his great curved beak, tearing out a handful of black and yellow hair.

Now the jaguar stopped, for this was too much. And as the toucan bird came diving down again, the jaguar lashed out at him with both his sharp clawed paws, one, two, with lightning swiftness. But not swiftly enough, for the impudent bird rose into the air untouched, cawing derisively in his loud hoarse voice. And he dived at him once more and then flew up and sat on a branch high above the great cat's head.

The jaguar glared at him angrily for a moment, but then he realized that he could never catch his winged enemy. And he remembered the little animal he had been chasing, and stared down the path again—but the vicuña had vanished. The jaguar sniffed at the ground till he

picked up the trail, and began to follow it, at first creeping slowly, but then trotting more and more swiftly—till he looked up: And there on the trail before him was a round little animal encased in armor plates. It was the armadillo, and he was sitting right in the middle of the jungle path, looking at the jaguar inquisitively.

The jaguar stopped and crouched. His tail lashed back and forth furiously, now he was tremendously angry—and tremendously hungry. He leaped at the little round animal in one great leap, and the armadillo turned and scurried away like a streak. The jaguar pounced after him, and again Xingu and the sloth began to fear that he would catch one of their friends, and began pelting him with nuts. But in just the last moment the armadillo turned off the trail and dived down into the deep hole which he had dug under a tree trunk. And the jaguar stood there, glaring at the hole, and the little animal peered up at him from the bottom of it—and there was nothing at all the jaguar could do.

Finally the jaguar turned away, and he began pacing back and forth in the jungle, growling with rage and frustration. Then he remembered the nuts with which he had been pelted, and he looked up into the tree tops, with the rage burning yellow in his great cat's eyes—and he found Xingu and the sloth sitting up on their high perch.

Then the jaguar crouched under their tree, and his tail lashed back and forth like a whip, and his low growling seemed to shake the very roots of the high tree, till the thick trunk trembled.

And suddenly he leaped, and came swarming up the trunk of the tree, and he climbed swiftly from branch to branch, higher and higher, and nearer and nearer. And Xingu grew more and more frightened, as he saw the jaguar's eyes burning at him with such deadly fury and the sharp white fangs bared, coming closer—

"Don't worry, he will never be able to get up here," the sloth reassured him, in his slow sleepy voice. "Are you sure?" Xingu asked, his own voice trembling and not at all convinced. For the great beast was terribly close indeed, almost up to their own height now, creeping along a slender branch, inching closer. And it seemed to Xingu that he could almost feel the great cat's hot breath, and he drew his feet up onto his branch—

Then suddenly there was a tremendous crackling sound, and the branch on which the jaguar was crouching bent, and then broke clean off— And the great cat went hurtling down to the ground, clawing at the empty air and yelling. And he hit the ground with a thud—though, being a cat, he had managed to get all his four padded paws under him. Therefore he was not really much the worse for his dizzy fall, though he crouched there stunned for a little while—

"You see," said the sloth phlegmatically— "He should never have tried that. But he was filled with rage, and rage makes one foolish. It is also very tiring—" And the sloth yawned a great yawn.

The jaguar below rose, shook himself, glared up at the tree once more, and then with a scream of anger and disappointment, went bounding off into the jungle.

"I think in a little while it will be quite safe to go down," said the sloth, "for he has gone to some other part of the forest to look for his dinner. Do you think you can get back down to the ground all right by yourself?"

"I think so," said Xingu.

"Then if you will pardon me," said the sloth, with another tremendous yawn, "I think I will catch up on some of the sleep I have lost, for I am very tired—" And he had hardly finished speaking before he was fast asleep.

Slowly and carefully Xingu climbed down from the top of the great tree. It took him quite a while, and he was very relieved when he felt the solid ground under his feet again.

Meanwhile all the other animals had returned, and were gathered chattering excitedly about the great adventure. They were all jubilant and triumphant about the way they had outwitted the jaguar—but it had been a very close thing indeed.

Then Xingu suddenly noticed how the rays of the sun were slanting through the trees, the sun was already low on the Western horizon. "O dear," he exclaimed, "it has become so late, and my mother will be waiting for me, and will be very worried!"

"Let us go quickly then," said Liniani, and after bidding good-bye to their friends, he and Xingu hurried home through the jungle.

It was already quite dark when Xingu approached his parents' hut in the clearing. He had never been away so late before and he was afraid of what they would say to him. And when he stepped into the hut, there were his father and his mother by the fire, and they both were looking at him as he entered—

"I am terribly sorry, dear parents," Xingu said quickly—"but I was playing down by the river, and I'm afraid I did not notice how late it had become, till I saw the sun setting—"

He had decided it would be better not to speak of his great adventure, though he really wanted very much to tell his father how he had helped his friends outwit the terrible jaguar. But he feared that when his mother heard what danger he had been in, she would not let him go into the jungle any more—

"You should have come home sooner, you must never stay away till after sunset, Xingu," his father said very sternly—"for it makes your mother very troubled and anxious."

"O, there is really nothing to worry about, mother," Xingu said.

"But I do worry, and I don't like it at all, and you must never stay away so late again!" said his mother, and Xingu saw that she was really very angry.

"But we won't scold him any more on this day," the father said, placating her, and then turned to Xingu with a big smile— "Happy birthday, my son!"

And the mother, forgetting her anger, came and took him in her arms, and said: "Happy birthday, dear Xingu!"

And then she went to one of her baskets in the corner and took out a new shirt of beautifully painted bark, which she had made for Xingu, and gave it to him. Xingu had never seen such a beautiful shirt and he put it on right away and said: "Now if we go to the village again, all the other children will envy me, for none of them have a shirt nearly so nice as this."

And then the father went to the place where he kept his weapons, which Xingu was never allowed to touch, and from beneath the rest he took a small bow and a quiver full of arrows he had hidden there. He came to Xingu with the bow and arrows in his hands and looked at him solemnly. And Xingu felt that his heart was beating very strongly.

"You are now old enough, my son, to begin learning the art of the hunter," Japura the father said— "Here is a bow which I have made, and some arrows. They are yours." And with that he gave the bow and arrows to Xingu.

The boy was so overjoyed, that at first he could not speak at all, but just stood, looking at the weapons in his hands. And he still could not quite believe it and said to his father: "They are for me, they are really for me?"

And the father said: "Yes, my boy, they are yours."

"O thank you, father!" Xingu cried.

But then the mother said: "Put them away now, and come and eat your supper, for it is really very late."

Reluctantly Xingu put the bow and arrows down by his hammock, and sat by the fire. And though his mother kept telling him to eat slowly, or else he would have a stomach ache later in the night, still Xingu wolfed down his food as quickly as he could, in order to be finished and go back to his wonderful present as soon as possible. And the moment he had swallowed the last bite, he ran and fetched the bow—

"It is a good strong bow," the father said, "let us see whether you can bend it—" And Japura showed him how to string the bow putting the bowstring in the notch at one end, and then bending the bow so that the string could be fitted in the notch at the other end. And though it was indeed a fine strong bow, Xingu found, after the first two or three attempts, that he could bend it and string it himself. And when the bow was strung, Xingu pulled back the bowstring, almost to his face, the way he had seen his father do, and then let it snap back with a twang.

But his father would not let him fit an arrow to the string— "Never do that inside the hut," Japura told him —"for you may break something, or even hurt somebody. Tomorrow morning we will go out in the clearing, and I will teach you how to shoot."

Xingu was so excited that he lay in the hammock and could not sleep for a long time—and therefore of course the night seemed much longer. But finally he went to sleep, and when he woke up the first rays of the morning sun were just coming through the entrance of the hut.

As soon as they had finished breakfast the father and Xingu went out into the clearing in front of the hut. And his father showed him how to hold the bow in the right way, and how to fit the arrow to the string, and draw it back toward his ear, sighting at the same time along the length of the arrow, and how to release it so that it would fly straight and not be deflected from its path. Then Japura picked out a tree trunk at the edge of the clearing, that had a big knothole at which Xingu could aim, and then paced back from it to the place where they would stand to shoot—not too far away at first.

And then Xingu drew back the bowstring and for the first time loosed an arrow. But the first shot went down into the ground at his feet, and the second went high up into the branches of the tree, and Xingu had to climb up to fetch the arrow back down again. But gradually it went better, and the fifth arrow only missed the tree trunk by an arm's length, and on the twentieth shot Xingu actually hit the tree. Then he felt very proud, as though he were already a skilled archer. And his father showed him how to raise his aim for greater distance, and how to shoot a little to one side to allow for the wind, and when they stopped at noontime, Xingu had twice hit the knothole. And his father praised him, and said that he had shot very well for the first time, and that if he practised every day, he would be a fine hunter when he grew up.

In the afternoon the father took his nets and his trident, and went fishing on the river. And as soon as he had left,

Xingu said to his mother that he was going to play at the edge of the clearing, and took his bow and his arrows and ran off. He ran straight into the jungle, looking for his friends, so that he could show them the wonderful present his father had given him, and the new thing he had learned. And he was so excited and proud, that he ran and skipped and jumped all the way.

He had not gone very far, when he saw his friend Liniani coming down the forest path.

Xingu ran towards him, and when he came nearer, held up his bow and cried: "Look, look, what I have! Look at me, look!" and then he fitted an arrow to the string and drew it back, pointing it straight at the vicuña, and cried: "Watch out, Liniani, watch out—for I am a mighty hunter now, watch out!" And he let fly the arrow which missed the vicuña by only a handsbreadth—

And Liniani stood there, looking at him with big eyes, and could not believe what he saw—and when the arrow whistled past, he did not move, he was so astonished at what Xingu was doing, he could not believe that his friend was really shooting at him. And he stood quite still, while Xingu fitted a second arrow to his bow, shouting again, full of pride and excitement: "Watch out, I'm a mighty hunter!"

And Xingu aimed more carefully this time, and the sharp arrow grazed Liniani's shoulder, stinging and sear-

ing him like a hot iron. Then the vicuña turned quickly, and ran away as fast as his legs could carry him.

And while he ran, Liniani was wondering what had happened to Xingu, and why he was behaving in such a strange way, shouting so wildly and fiercely, and why he had such a cruel gleam in his eyes, and why he was trying to hurt him, and shot at him. And he ran a little way through the jungle, and then dodged behind a big tree, and stuck out his head just a little, and peered back to see what Xingu was doing now.

Xingu was coming after him, plunging through the jungle growth, and he still had that wild excited look in his face and was shouting: "Now I shall track you through the jungle, Liniani, for I am a mighty hunter and I shall track you down!"

And when he saw the vicuña peering out at him from behind the tree, he stopped and fitted another arrow to his bow and loosed it quickly, and it came whistling straight for Liniani's head. But this time the vicuña was forewarned, he pulled his head back quickly and the arrow whizzed past him. Then he turned and scurried off through the trees.

Xingu hurried after him, eagerly following his trail, hunting him. Then he saw him stop again, far ahead, and the little animal waited, until Xingu was almost near enough to try another shot. But as soon as he started to raise his bow, Liniani was off again, nimbly and swiftly he leaped over roots and low branches and the thick creepers. Till Xingu could barely see him far in the distance, darting between the great trees. Then the vicuña stopped again, and waited, till the boy was almost within bowshot, and then ran on. And Liniani ran to the right, and Xingu after him, and then to the left, and Xingu still after him, and then straight ahead again. And he always stopped and waited, but he would never let Xingu get close enough to shoot again.

And that way they went deeper and deeper into the jungle. And Xingu was so filled with the eagerness of the chase and the wild excitement, that he was not watching where they were going at all—he was not paying attention to anything but the slender shape darting ahead of him, and then standing quite still and tensed, and then darting away again.

Till suddenly Liniani vanished. Xingu had just seen him the instant before, had seen him quite clearly standing between the trees, and then he had vanished, completely, as though the earth had swallowed him up. And Xingu went on more slowly, looking to the right and looking to the left and looking everywhere around him —but he could not see any sign of the vicuña. And he went to the spot where he had last seen the vicuña stand, and searched the ground for tracks, but he couldn't find

any among the twisting roots and the tangled undergrowth. And no matter how hard he looked, running
back and forth through the jungle, and searching everywhere, he could not find him. And then slowly he realized that perhaps he had frightened his friend by shooting at him, and he began to call out as loud as he could:
"Come back, Liniani, come back, little vicuña—I did not
really mean to hurt you, I was only playing, please come
back!"

But there was no answer, no sound at all, except the
wind rustling through the tops of the tall trees.

Then Xingu began to grow frightened. But he said to
himself: "I will walk through the jungle—I have so many
friends in the jungle. I will just walk a little way, and
surely I will meet one of them."

And he looked about, trying to decide which way to
go, but now the jungle, in which he had grown to feel so
at home, looked strange and dark and hostile. And he
thought, this must be a part of the forest in which he had
never been before. So he just walked straight ahead, and
to keep himself from being frightened, he repeated to
himself every few steps, that in just a few minutes he
would surely meet one of his friends. And he looked up
at the branches for his friend the sloth, and in the undergrowth for his friends the peccary and the tapir, and he
looked into the hole under the roots for his friend the

armadillo—but they were not there. There was no one.

The whole forest was still and empty. Not even the monkeys were chattering in the trees, and there was not even the distant call of the trumpet bird. And Xingu began to call his friends, one by one, by their names. But there was no answer, just the echoing of his voice among the tall trees, growing quickly fainter, dying away, and then the silence.

And Xingu grew more and more frightened. And he walked slowly through the strange and empty jungle, not really knowing where he was, or where he was going, and he felt more and more miserable all the time.

And he was so unhappy, and he was so frightened and worried, that he forgot all the things he had learned— even to look where he was going, and to watch carefully all around him. So that it was almost too late, when suddenly, out of the very corner of his eyes, he felt, rather than saw, a slight movement overhead—and he leaped back just in the last instant, as the big, thick coils lashed out at him from overhead. And the sinuous, mottled length of the anaconda whipped so near him, that just for a second he felt its cold leathery skin brush against his shoulder, and he staggered back. And if he had come just one step further, it would have caught him and encircled him in its powerful coils.

Then Xingu turned and ran, as he had never run before in his life. He ran wildly and in panic through the jungle, ran with his heart choking in his throat, ran till his breath came in desperate gasps, yet dared not to stop. Till at last, stumbling over a root, he tumbled headlong onto the ground. But in his fear he was up as quickly as he had gone down, and he stood there trembling in every limb, and he could run no farther.

He looked around. The shadows of the jungle had grown much deeper—the sun was setting. Darkness was falling, and he could no longer see clearly. And as night falls very quickly in those regions, in a few moments he could not see anything at all. And he was too terrified to move, for fear of what might be lying in wait for him, invisible in the jungle night.

Then, shaking and weak, he dropped down at the foot of a great tree, and crouched down, shivering, between the thick roots at its base. And he felt so lost and lonely, and more frightened than he had ever imagined he could be—and he began to sob bitterly, crouching there in the night between the roots of the great tree.

At last great weariness, from all his wandering and running in the jungle, overcame him and he cried himself to sleep.

He woke up suddenly and full of fear, in the middle of the night. The full moon was high in the sky, and the small patch of open ground in front of him was aglow with its milky light. But the deep shadows of the trees all around were black and purple and quite impenetrable. And someone was watching him, hidden in those shadows.

Then a long bulky shape lumbered out into the moonlight. And then another, still bigger—and they were all converging upon him, till they were quite near. Then they sat down in a half circle around him, and looked at him.

Then Xingu saw that the first bulky shape was the anteater, and the second big one the tapir, and the slender shape was the vicuña, and the two smaller ones were the peccary and the armadillo. And they all sat in a half circle,

facing him in the moonlight, and looked at him in silence: the anteater severely and sternly, down his long nose; and the tapir with anger growing in his small eyes; and the peccary rather frightened and worried, and the armadillo with curiosity and astonishment, as though he had never seen anything like Xingu before. But the vicuña looked at him with great and reproachful sadness in his soft brown eyes.

Then the anteater said, in a stern voice: "So this is Xingu, the mighty hunter!"

And the tapir said: "So this is Xingu, who tracks his quarry through the jungle!"

And the peccary said: "Xingu, who hunts with the bow and sharp arrows!"

And the armadillo said: "Yes, yes, look, he is still holding the bow, and those are certainly arrows he has in that quiver!"

And then they looked at him in silence again.

And then the anteater said, and his deep voice was sterner and colder than ever: "So this is Xingu, who shoots at his friends!"

And the vicuña said, very softly: "Yes, that is he."

And the anteater said: "Xingu, who wounded his best friend with a cruel arrow!"

And the vicuña said so softly that one could barely hear him: "Yes, it is true."

64

Then the anteater said: "Step forward, Liniani—"

And the vicuña stepped forward, so that the moonlight fell upon his shoulder, and there was a long streak of dark red blood, which had flowed down from the wound the arrow had made there—

And the tapir cried out to Xingu in a loud fierce voice: "Look what you have done!"

But Liniani only looked at Xingu with large reproachful eyes.

Then the anteater asked: "Who showed Xingu the secret trails of the jungle?"

And Liniani said: "We did."

And the anteater asked: "Who showed him which berries were good to eat, and which make you sick?"

And the tapir said: "We did."

And the anteater asked: "And who showed him how to look out for the anaconda lying hidden in the branches, and the poisonous snakes beneath the ferns?"

And the armadillo said: "We did."

And the anteater asked: "Who showed him how to climb the highest trees to escape from the jaguar's claws?"

And a sleepy voice from above said: "We."

And Xingu looked up and saw the sloth hanging from a branch overhead—

Then the anteater said: "So we showed him all the ways of the jungle, and now he comes, and says he is a mighty hunter, and shoots at us, who were his friends and taught him all he knows—"

And the peccary exclaimed: "But why should he ever do a thing like that?"

And the armadillo said: "But didn't you hear, he is a mighty hunter now—"

And the tapir said: "Yes—like the jaguar, he hunts in the jungle, eager to kill—now silence walks before him, and fear creeps beside him, and all the smaller animals who were his friends must now flee from him—like the jaguar, he is our enemy now!"

Then the anteater asked: "What shall we do with him? What shall we do with Xingu who was our friend, but has now turned against us?"

Then the white eared marmoset swung from the lowest branch and cried in his high chattering voice: "Throw him in the river, so that the piranha fish can chew him to bits, bring him to the big snake so that he can swallow him whole, put him in an ant hill, so that the white ants will nibble at his bones!"

But they paid no attention to the marmoset and his chatter, and the anteater asked once more: "What shall we do with him?"

And then he turned to the boy: "Tell me, Xingu, what do you think we should do with you?"

Then Xingu said: "I did not mean it, I did not mean to

66

hurt him—Liniani is the best friend I have, I did not want to do him any harm, really and truly I didn't—I was just playing."

And Xingu looked at the vicuña, pleading that he should understand. But the vicuña had lowered his eyes to the ground, and would not look at him.

And the anteater asked: "What did you think, when you shot at Liniani—surely you must have realized that your arrow might hurt him?"

Then Xingu said, very ashamed: "I did not think—I was so excited and proud because my father gave me a bow and arrow for my birthday—I'm afraid I did not think at all—I did not think that it could hurt him—"

"But now you see that you have," said the tapir.

And Xingu said, "Yes—"

And the anteater said: "And if your arrow had gone just a little more to one side, Liniani might never have run and jumped and played and laughed any more—Liniani would have lain quite still and never moved again—do you realize that?"

And Xingu said, with the tears coming into his eyes: "Yes, I realize that now, but I would not want that to ever happen, you know that I wouldn't. I see now, that I have been very bad, and I am terribly sorry for what I have done." And he turned to the vicuña: "You must believe me, Liniani, I really am sorry—"

Then Liniani looked at him, and said gently: "Yes I believe you, Xingu."

And Xingu said: "I promise, I will never do anything like that again!"

But the tapir said: "He may be sorry now, but how can we be sure he will not do the same thing again later on?"

"No!" Xingu cried. "No! I will not do it again, ever. I did not know—"

"He is a man now," said the tapir dubiously, shaking his head.

"I am your friend," Xingu said, "and I know now that one must not hurt one's friends!"

There was a pause, and they all looked at him, for what seemed to Xingu like a terribly long time. And then the tapir turned to the others and asked: "Well, what shall we do with him?"

"I suppose," the anteater said quietly, "we had better take him home now—"

Then suddenly Xingu was terribly afraid and he ran to Liniani, and stood in front of him with pleading eyes— "We are still friends, Liniani, aren't we? We can still be friends?"

And the vicuña said: "Yes, Xingu, we are still friends—"

And Xingu turned around and looked at the others—

68

And they all nodded and for the first time they smiled at him. And Xingu was so happy and relieved that the tears came into his eyes again.

Then Liniani said: "But we must take you home now, for it is almost dawn."

And indeed the first blue light was beginning to glow along the horizon—

And when they came to the edge of the forest at the clearing, Liniani said: "We did not forget the birthday of our friend Xingu—we have gifts for you too."

Then all the animals ran, and they brought the gifts which they had hidden among the high grasses and the thin ferns of the jungle—

The peccary brought what looked like thick roots, and laid them at Xingu's feet. "These are yams," he said, "and they are very good to eat, and if you put them in the ground, many more will grow."

And the armadillo brought another plant. "And these are sweet potatoes, and they are very good too, and grow in much the same way."

And the tapir brought a big round vegetable. "This is the pumpkin—it is very good, I assure you, and inside there are many small seeds, from which, if you plant them, many other pumpkins will grow."

And then some small hard objects dropped down from above, and when Xingu looked up, there was the sloth looking down at him— "Nuts," said the sloth. "Very nourishing and tasty. You must plant nut trees."

"I wanted to give you some ants, but Liniani did not think you would appreciate them," said the anteater. "But here are some berries I have picked for you—"

Then Liniani said: "Now if you plant all these things that should keep you busy, and you will always have enough to eat, and will never go hungry."

"Yes," said the armadillo, giggling— "For even the greatest hunter comes home empty handed at times."

Then Xingu looked at all the things they had brought him, and he looked at his friends—and when he thought how kind they were to him, the tears came into his eyes again. And he said: "Thank you, thank you so very much for all your wonderful gifts—and thank you for teaching me what it means to be friends—"

And Xingu picked up all his gifts, and went through the clearing to his parents' hut.

And the sun was rising over the dark green forest when Xingu came home—

When Xingu came into the hut his mother was sitting in a corner weeping, for since he had been gone all night she thought that something terrible had happened to him and that she would never see her son again.

But when Xingu said: "Mother," and she saw him standing there in the door of the hut, she rose to her feet

70

and stared at him for a moment, and then ran to him and took him in her arms—and then she started to weep all over again, but this time because she was so relieved and happy to have him back again.

And then Xingu asked, "Where is father?" And his mother said that his father had gone into the jungle to look for him, following his tracks.

And toward noon the father came back, saying, as he entered the hut, in a low, hopeless voice, "I lost the trail. I could not find him." But the mother cried: "Look, he is here, he has come back safe and sound—"

Then the father looked at Xingu, and then asked him to tell what had happened to him.

Then Xingu told his father he had gone hunting into the jungle yesterday and had lost his way, and how all the animals had come to him at night—and then he showed his father all the things the animals had given him: the yams and sweet potatoes and pumpkins and nuts.

And then Xingu took the bow and arrows and gave them back to his father and said to him in a solemn voice: "I shall never be a hunter, father, for the animals of the jungle are my friends. Instead I shall cultivate the earth and make all these good things grow in it."

And the father looked at him in astonishment, and thought that this son of his, who would not be a hunter, was a very strange son indeed. But then he looked at all the things which his son had brought back, and thought that one to whom the animals gave such gifts must have a very strong magic and must be a very powerful medicine man—so he did not say anything—

And when the first crop that Xingu planted in the clearing came up, and they had plenty to eat, even when the other hunters of the tribe came back with empty hands, having shot nothing at all, then Xingu's parents were very proud of him and so was the whole tribe. They thought that he was wiser than any man of the Amazon valley had ever been.